Please, Miss!

Tony Bradman

Illustrated by Priscilla Lamont

CAMBRIDGE
UNIVERSITY PRESS

"Please, Miss! Can I sharpen the pencils?"
said Sarah.

"Of course you can," said Miss Miller, smiling.

But that's when the trouble began.

Sarah sharpened the pencils . . . but she
did it too well.

"Please, Miss! Can I water the plants?"
said Sarah.

"Only if you're careful," said Miss Miller.

But Sarah watered the plants . . .
too much.

"Please, Miss! Can I put the paint pots out?" said Sarah.

"Only if you're careful," said Miss Miller.

But Sarah put the paint pots out . . .
too quickly.

"Please, Miss! Can I tidy the toys away?"
said Sarah.

"Only if you're careful," said Miss Miller.

But Sarah tidied the toys away . . .
too roughly.

"Please, Miss! Can I . . . ?" said Sarah.

"No, you can't," said Miss Miller.

"And I want to talk to you."

"I'm in trouble now!" thought Sarah.

But Miss Miller just wanted to show Sarah
the right way to do things.

It was easy-peasy!

"Please, Miss! Can I go and play?"
said Sarah, at last.

"Of course you can," said Miss Miller,
smiling again.

Then Sarah ran out of the classroom . . .
too fast!